NOTICE

This is *not*
a NORMAL book.

It is full of
CRAZY STUFF.

And DANGER.

You have
been warned.

P.S. If you sit down and read this book in
ONE GO, right now, the closest adult in the area
(parent, teacher, librarian,
walrus inspector, grobsnot breeder, etc.)
will give you a TREAT.

If you don't believe me, give it a try.

www.total-mayhem.com

Text and illustrations copyright © 2020
by Lisa Swerling & Ralph Lazar

This book is being published simultaneously in hardcover
by Scholastic Press.

All rights reserved. Published by Scholastic Inc., Publishers
since 1920. SCHOLASTIC, SCHOLASTIC PRESS, and associated logos
are trademarks and/or registered trademarks of Scholastic Inc.
First published by Last Lemon Productions in 2020.

The publisher does not have any control over and does
not assume any responsibility for author or third-party
websites or their content.

ISBN 978-1-338-77037-7

1 2021

Printed in the U.S.A.   23
First printing 2021

Book design by Lisa Swerling & Ralph Lazar

Boring stuff

Hole-digger
Aardvark 4.2d

TOTAL MAYHEM BOOK 1
MONDAY — INTO THE
CAVE OF THIEVES

Stalactites

CONTENTS

Created by Ralph Lazar.
Lovingly pummeled into
shape by Lisa Swerling.

Absolutely
no idea what
this is

Stalagmites

SCHOLASTIC INC.

Things you need to know before you start reading this book:

ABOUT DASH

Full Name: Dash Candoo
Age: 11 years old
School: Swedhump Elementary
Best Friend: Rob Newman
Favorite Meal: Breakfast
Favorite Drink: Wombat juice
Weapon of Choice: Stink-ball
Vehicle of Choice: Hole-digger
Favorite Class: Paper Airplanes
Favorite Teacher: Mr. Hogsbottom
Favorite Sport: Wobble-ball

NATO Code Name: Delta Alpha Sierra Hotel
Morse Code Name: -../.-/ ... /....

ABOUT THE ALMANAC

There are SO MANY new and interesting and weird things in Dash's world that there's a whole section about them at the back of this book, called the Almanac.

The **Book 1** Almanac documents everything that appears in this story: Vehicles, Communications, Weapons, Scallywags, Activities, Food, Animals, Trees, Plants, Schools, and more!

So if you see an **underlined** word, like <u>grobsnot</u>, flip to the back for more info.

The **complete** Almanac is the place to find out EVERYTHING about Dash and his world.

It's online here: **total-mayhem.com/almanac**

CHARACTERS

Into the Cave of Thieves

Wrestle-Scallywags
Enemy fighters

Mrs. Hogmanny-Hog-Mahomm
Vegetables teacher

Dash Candoo
Hero of these stories

Rob Newman
Dash's best friend

Mrs. Belch-Hick
English teacher

Mr. Darling
Math teacher

Gronville Honkersmith
Classmate

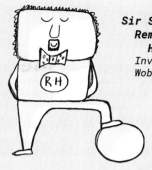

Sir Stephenson Remington-Hobbes
Inventor of Wobble-Ball

Mr. Hogsbottom
Paper Airplane teacher

Devil-Cat
Enemy fighter

Name unknown
Substitute teacher

Mr. Grodzinsky
PE/Wobble-Ball teacher

Jeanjean-Jeanjean-Jeanjean Johnson
Classmate, twin of Jonjon

Mrs. Tadros
Science teacher

Jonjon-Jonjon-Jonjon Johnson
Classmate, twin of Jeanjean

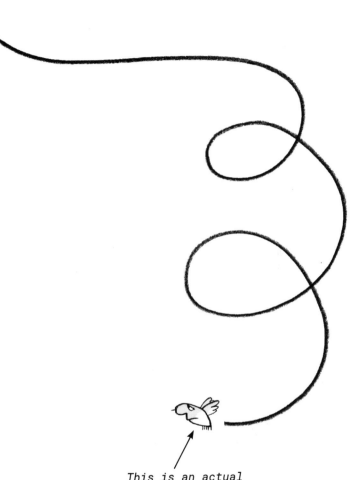

This is an actual
grobsnot, in case you
were wondering.

Chapter 1

Before Breakfast

It REALLY annoys me when one gets into a
Total Mayhem Situation
before breakfast.

Which is exactly what happened to me this morning.

I had just poured
myself a glass of
fresh <u>wombat juice</u> and
was sitting down to a
bowl of cereal when
my **KB-15** started
flashing **red.**

As you probably know,
a red flashing KB-15 means
DANGER IS VERY CLOSE!!

I didn't even have
time to prepare.

I went straight to the
front door, opened it,
and there I saw them.

Three combat-ready <u>scallywags</u>.

And not just any old scallywags.

<u>Wrestle-Scallywags</u>!
The most agile scallywags around.

And beside them was the
**two-tailed
<u>Devil-Cat</u>!**

I knew immediately that
this was
NOT
a good situation
because:

[a] I was still
in my pajamas,

[b] I was outnumbered,

[c] I was still holding
my bowl of cereal,

and [d]

actually I
can't remember
what [d] was.

I've been in a lot of
situations with the
two-tailed Devil-Cat
before.

He is very, *very*,
very, very, very,
very, very, very,
very,very, very, very,
very, **very**, very,
very, very dangerous

and you need to move
calmly yet
super quickly,
which is what I did.

I activated my
<u>transformer</u>
(which I always
have on me).

This transformed
my cereal bowl

into a
watermelon,

which I
hurled
straight at
Devil-Cat.

Perfectly on target,
the watermelon got
stuck in his mouth and
he was out of the game,
for now.

If you have a
watermelon in your
mouth, there's not much
you can do about it.

Next, the scallywags.
I have had over
345 encounters
with Wrestle-Scallywags,
and I know you need to
act fast.

These ones were
ready to fight.

And as you may know from

the **Almanac**,
Wrestle-Scallywags
master over **27,004**
different moves each.

So theoretically I had faced
81,012
different moves.

And while I know
the Almanac
well, I don't
know every
single move.

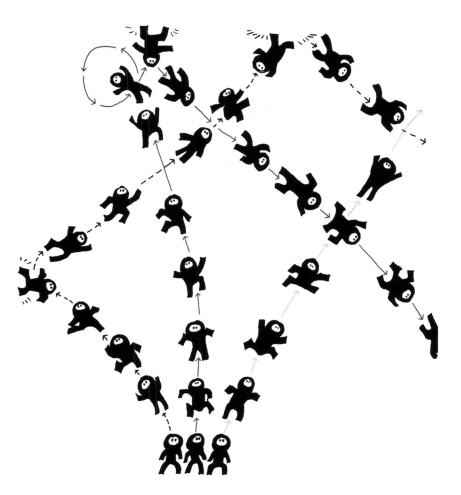

They immediately
went into

Move #6694
(Tower)

which is a
very
dangerous

three-against-one
configuration.

So I reactivated
my transformer

to change the ground
between us into
quicksand.

"WHY QUICKSAND?!"
I hear you ask.

Unfortunately I don't have
time to explain my **every
move** when I'm in a
Total Mayhem Situation.
Sorry.

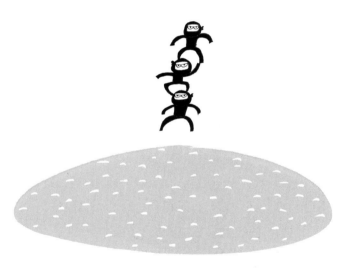

The Wrestle-Scallywags
began to advance.

But they didn't see
the quicksand and...

...game over.

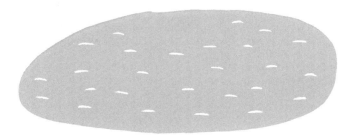

I went back inside and poured myself another bowl of cereal.

And that's how
my day started.

It was kind of annoying.

With no wombat juice, plus
I had to eat my cereal
really fast. But that's
what you have to deal with
when you are me.

Chapter 2

Vegetables

So after breakfast I got
changed, packed my bag,
and went off to my school
Swedhump Elementary.

On the way to school there
were no incidents.

No combat incidents, I mean.
And certainly no
Total Mayhem Situations.

Then I saw my best
friend, Rob Newman.

He asked if I wanted to
have a quick game of
<u>paper-rock-scissors-
carrot-spoon-tissue-
elbow</u>.

It's a complicated game
and I don't have time to
explain it right now.

I told him I did, but just for five minutes since I didn't want to be late for **Vegetables**, my first class of the day. I love this class mainly because of _Carrot 27b_.

Rob laughed at me.

"You LOVE that carrot!"
he said with a smile.

So true.

We played one round.
Rob won, but I
didn't mind.

And then I headed off to
the school's vegetable
garden.

Mrs. Hogmanny-Hog-Mahomm
is our Vegetables
teacher.

She teaches us:

[1] how to **grow** vegetables, and

[2] how to speak the main vegetable **languages.**

It is said that she speaks
over **three hundred** different
vegetable languages.

Also, she is
WORLD FAMOUS
for

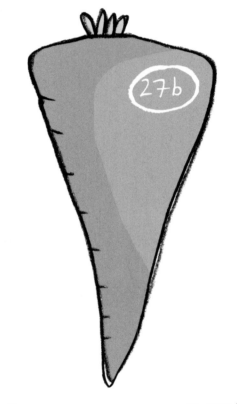

Carrot 27b.

There are three things you need to know about **this epic vegetable:**

[1] Mrs. Hogmanny-Hog-Mahomm planted it.

[2] It's the **world's largest** carrot.

[3] I **LOVE** carrots, so it's very important to me.

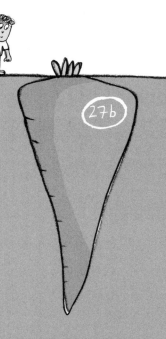

For today's lesson
we were learning
Broccolish (you can
guess which vegetable
speaks that).

If you speak any Broccolish,
all I can say to you is
brrrrghhh-kkkf-kfff, with
some chocolate on top,
please.

Toward the end of the
lesson, I became aware of
some movement behind me.

I turned around to see soil
flying out of the ground
around Carrot 27b.

How totally weird.

Dirt flying **everywhere** but
nothing actually *digging*.

At least, nothing
visible.

Was it something *in*visible?

I took my _anti-invisibility goggles_ out of my backpack and put them on.

I could not
believe my eyes!

There, right there, was
Devil-Cat, trying to
dig out Carrot 27b.

I had to act, and I had
to act FAST!

I activated the anti-invisibility goggles' built-in <u>VAMP transponder</u>.

This turned my voice into the voice of **Devil-Cat's mother.**

I ran for him yelling as loud as I could.

And boy, did it work!

Devil-Cat dropped his
spade and **ran** for his
life.

He must be truly
terrified of his mom.

But Mrs. Hogmanny-Hog-Mahomm
and the rest of the class
were staring at me

as if, indeed, I was
completely out of control.

Luckily, right then
the bell rang and it
was the end of the
lesson.

A big relief, because
it was going to be
hard to explain to
everyone that I was
chasing away an
invisible cat.

Chapter 3

Wobble-Ball

Next up was
<u>Wobble-Ball</u> class.

I don't mind Wobble-Ball,
but the problem is that
it's in the gym building.

The floor of the gym
building is really hard,
which means:

[a] it is often cold, and

[b] it's hard to dig
through, so you can't really
ESCAPE if you need to.

In a lot of my other classes, I have quite effective ways of escaping. For example, in my English class, where the floor is not quite as hard, I've got a trapdoor under my desk, which leads to three tunnels that I made. And those tunnels go pretty far.

Tunnel **Alpha** goes to the school's orange grove.

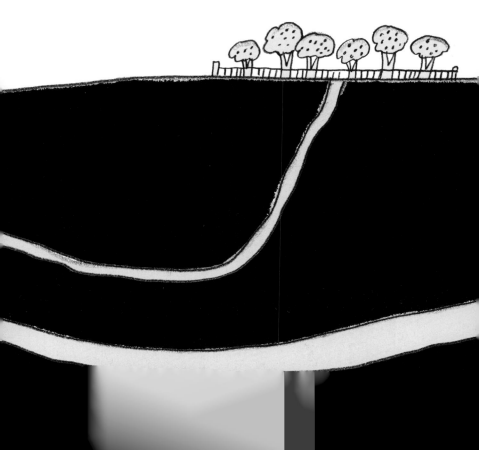

Tunnel **Beta** goes
back to my house.

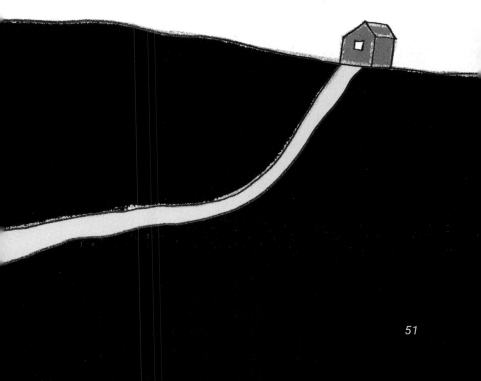

And Tunnel **Charlie** is **really** deep and I don't want to tell you about it now because it will probably scare you.

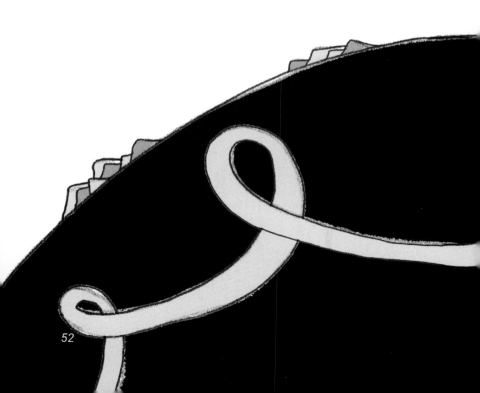

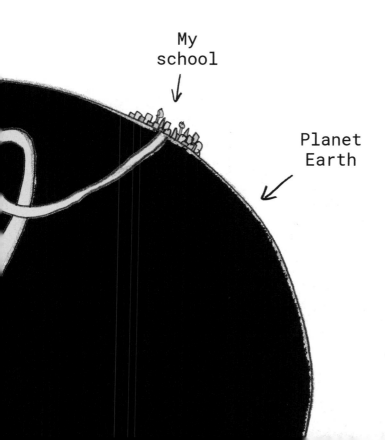

My
school

Planet
Earth

Anyway, back to
Wobble-Ball class.

Mr. Grodzinsky is our
Wobble-Ball instructor,
and there are two
things you need to
know about him:

[1] He has been the
**WORLD Wobble-Ball
CHAMPION** for the last
three years, so he is
really famous.

[2] It is rumored that he is **totally bald** but wears a wig, and has a tattoo of a dancing aardvark right on the top of his head.

As reigning World
Wobble-Ball Champion,
Mr. Grodzinsky
is holder of the
Remington-
Hobbes Trophy.
It's made of solid gold!

It lives in its own
special, highly secure,
bulletproof cabinet
in the gym, which is
attached to the floor
on a dynamite-proof
concrete plinth.

BULLETPROOF
GLASS →

WORLD
#1

STOT
INKI

↑ DYNAMITE-
PROOF
CONCRETE

Mr. Grodzinsky
polishes the cabinet
at least twice a day.

As everyone knows,
the Remington-Hobbes
Trophy is named after
Sir Stephenson
Remington-Hobbes,
inventor of Wobble-Ball.

We have a **massive** poster
of him in the gym.

He was World Champion
for the first four years.

But in the fifth year, he
lost the trophy to
Mr. Grodzinsky, who has
won the competition every
year since.

Our school is also very
proud of winning the
Stotinki Trophy for the
Best-Smelling Gym
in the District.

Because it's made of
regular silver (and not
pure gold), it's not
behind bulletproof
glass or anything.

That's all the info
about the trophies...
but I can hear you
asking, **"What actually
is Wobble-Ball?"**

Good question!

It's a sport that involves racing around a room while balancing atop a big, wobbly rubber ball.

It's **FUN**, but also quite **DIFFICULT!**

And what do we do in
Wobbble-Ball class?

We race!

The first race was
going well, with Rob
in the lead and me
just behind him.

I HAD to overtake him!

Meanwhile, Gronville Honkersmith, who is very fast, was catching up...

...but then he crashed into Jonjon-Jonjon-Jonjon Johnson, which was quite funny.

Jeanjean-Jeanjean-Jeanjean Johnson (Jonjon-Jonjon-Jonjon's twin sister) had just begun closing in on me when my **KB-15** started flashing.

SUDDENLY
Devil-Cat appeared out of **nowhere.**

Mr. Grodzinsky got such
a fright that his hair
went flying off and
landed on Gronville
Honkersmith's face
like some kind of
**hairy, face-sucking
leech thing.**

In the confusion,
Devil-Cat grabbed the
Stotinki Trophy and
ran out the gym door!

Rob and I looked at each
other and knew it was
time for **action!**

We grabbed our backpacks
and pulled out
our trusty **quadcycles.**

We headed off in
hot pursuit.

We closed in
on our target.
Devil-Cat was
ducking and
diving.

Rob tried to down him
with a volley of
stink-balls,
but Devil-Cat swerved
just in time.

I tried a few
yo-yo stingers,
but Devil-Cat swatted
them away like flies.

Fearing I was out of
options, I reached into
my bag and realized,
to my delight, that
my <u>backpack-ladder</u>
was in there.

Deployment activated!

Devil-Cat fell
with a
bang.

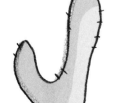

The watermelon
exploded into a
million tiny pieces.

In the chaos,
Devil-Cat went into
invisible mode (not
again!) and escaped
with the trophy.

Not much to be done,
for now at least.

So Rob and I
sped back to our
Wobble-Ball class.

 , , ,

Back at school, the
wig was still stuck
to Gronville's face.

He was making weird
turtle noises, and we
didn't want to hang
around.

When we told Mr. Grodzinsky
that the Stotinki Trophy
had not been recovered, he
burst into tears. We vowed
to find it for him.

Then the bell rang;
time for the next
class. It was **math**,
and for that we could
not be late.

Chapter 4
Math

Math is taught by Mr. Darling.

Despite his last name,
he is *weirdly strict*,
which is why it's not
worth being late.

Mr. Darling is obsessed with his <u>pinkfish</u>, and every day during recess, he takes them for a walk around the schoolyard...

...and then usually reads them a story.

Gronville Honkersmith
was once late and as
punishment had to walk the
pinkfish. It was very
embarrassing for him.

I'd decided earlier that it was too risky to tell you about my escape tunnel from math class, so I didn't even mention it. But now that I know you a bit better, I think I'm okay to share. But please don't tell anyone.

It starts under the potted plant...

...and then heads
down to my SCC
(*Secure Command Center*).
Rob is the only other
person who knows about it.

I'll tell him I've
told you.

It's also connected to
some of my other tunnels.
But more about that
another day.

So there we were
in math class.
Mr. Darling was busy
telling us about what
he'd done over the
weekend with his fish.

They'd gone on a hike.

And they'd also gone
to the beach.

Deeply fascinating.

I couldn't get my mind
off Devil-Cat.

Could there be clues
to find the stolen
trophy at the spot
where he'd vanished?

When Mr. Darling turned
his back, I got up from
my desk without anyone
noticing, snuck over to
the potted plant, lifted
it up...

...and slipped
into the tunnel.

I had a plan.

Once in the SCC,
I activated a **drone**.

I sent it out across the open plain to where we'd last seen Devil-Cat.

The drone filmed
the area around
the cactus.

Nothing!

I then activated
the *infra-green*
camera.

And there, suddenly,
as clear as day,
I saw them!

Devil-Cat prints!

Devil-Cat's prints are VERY
difficult to spot because
he is so light-footed.

But there they were,
leading from the cactus
straight into the hills.

And from the hills...

...to a **cave!**

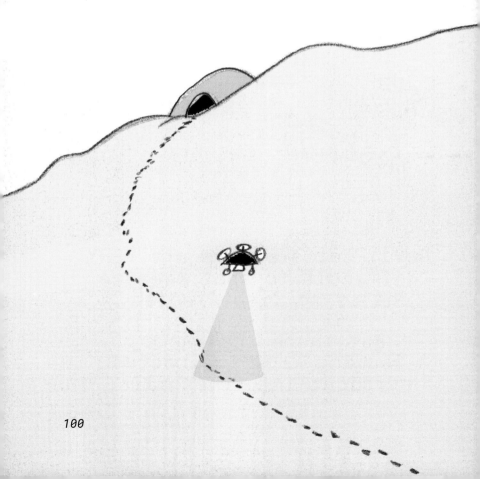

But now there was a new
danger — that Mr. Darling
would notice my absence.
Rob and I would have to
explore later. Right now
I had to get back to class.

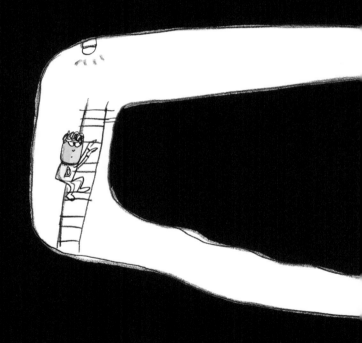

I set the drone to
return-to-base mode and
headed back up the tunnel.

Once I was safely back at my desk, my mind raced with questions.

Why had Devil-Cat been digging up Carrot 27b?

Why did he want the Stotinki Trophy?

What was hiding in that cave??!!

Then I heard my name
being called.

"Dash."

"Dash!"

It was
Mr. Darling.

And he was not happy.

"**Dash,** stop daydreaming!
And remain behind during
recess.

Someone's going to be
walking my babies.

And it's YOU!"

And I have to admit,
it was a little
embarrassing.

Chapter 5

Science

Recess ended.

Thankfully!

I took the fish back to
Mr. Darling, and then I was
off to the science lab.

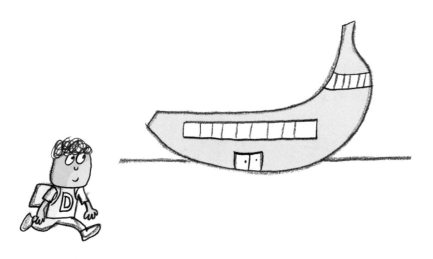

Don't ask me why
the science lab is shaped
like a banana because I
have no idea.

Mrs. Tadros is our science teacher and she's *amazing.*

Not only is she a brilliant teacher, but she is also famous for being able to make all kinds of *perfumes.*

Behind her desk
is a painting of
a palm tree,

and behind that
painting is a
hidden wall safe.

And in that wall safe
is a famous bottle
of perfume.

It's called
Egyptian Blue,
and Mrs. Tadros made it.

She had to travel in a
boat for a year along
the River Nile to
collect the ingredients.

It is said to be one of
the *most expensive*
bottles of perfume
on the planet!

But back to the main story:

Rob is in my science class, and I told him about the footprints to the cave.

We decided to see what
was going on in that
cave.

Mrs. Tadros is a very
relaxed teacher, so I
asked her if Rob and I
could take a five-minute
break because we needed
some fresh air.

She said okay.

Sure, no
problemo !

Because time was short,
Rob and I decided to use
the **warp-vortex**.

I can't tell you much
about it because it's
totally secret, but it's
kind of like a pipe
through the sky.

I removed the
warp-vortex input nozzle
from my backpack,we both said
the password (which I also
can't tell you, sorry),and...

...in a flash we were
sucked up...

...and deposited
at the cave entrance.

I strapped on my KB-15.

Right there I saw
a piece of paper on
the ground.

I picked it up and
was about to read
it when...

...my **KB-15** started flashing bright. **Really bright.** I pocketed the piece of paper just in time.

Because then — out of
nowhere — came a **Total
Wrestle-Scallywag
Attack!**

This one was serious.
Their initial move was
a **TYF-3332**.

We responded with a
Double-Helix-LL14.

They came back with an
MKB-2994,

followed by a
ZZ-12438.

And then
another **ZZ-12438,**
but this time
upside down.*

This is a famous and
very technical move.

* So technically
it was a
ZZ-12438.

Not good.

We were cornered!

Rob and I knew our only chance was a **_Full Mayhem Extrication using the warp-vortex._**

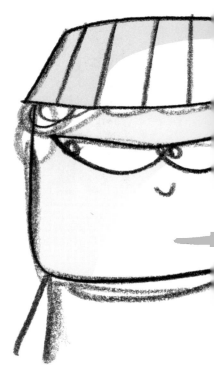

Just as the Wrestle-
Scallywags started their
final move, I released
the output nozzle from my
backpack, we both said the
password (which, again,
I can't tell you, so don't
even ask)...

...and **whoosh,**
we were gone.

In an instant, we were back on the blacktop at school.

We'd been away for exactly *four minutes* and *thirty-seven seconds*.

We heard panicky
voices coming from
the science lab.

Everyone was crowded
around Mrs. Tadros's
desk and she was crying.

The safe had been
broken open.

And the bottle of Egyptian Blue was **GONE!**

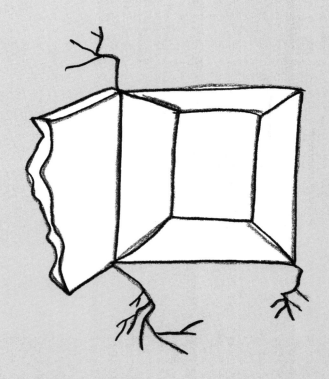

Chapter 6

English

Our next class was English.

This is our English teacher, **Mrs. Belch-Hick.**

She's a bit weird.

This is Dog, her cat.

If you didn't understand
that, let me say
it another way.

This is her cat, Dog.

She's named her cat Dog.

I told you she
was weird.

Dog is also a bit weird.
She can walk up walls
and often can be seen
sleeping on the
ceiling.

But no time to talk
about her now.

Today's lesson was poetry,
and today's poem was a
very, very, very, **VERY**
famous one about a man who
married a spoon.

But because of what had
just happened at the cave,
Rob and I were not really
able to concentrate on
the man, or the spoon,
or their marriage.

We needed to get back to
the cave.

What was going on?

I pulled a <u>freeze-bomb</u>
out of my backpack and
activated it.

Everyone in the room,
including Dog and
Mrs. Belch-Hick, froze.

We had fifteen minutes
(that's exactly how long
freeze-bombs work for —
and if you don't believe
me, check for yourself in
the ALMANAC).

Frozen
just as
she was
about to
start
reading

Frozen
scratching
his nose

Frozen
walking
up
wall

Frozen with
surprised
face

MBH

I don't know if you remember, but I told you about the tunnels under my desk in math class.

Rob and I quickly went down *Tunnel Alpha,* which leads to the orange grove.

The orange grove is
where we hide our
<u>hole-digger</u>.

We started it up and
were off...

...back to the cave!

141

143

At the entrance, we were
rewarded with the sight of
three Wrestle-Scallywags
just about to enter.

As we got closer, we
realized they were
carrying the
Egyptian Blue!

Thieves!

We quietly followed
them into the cave.

From our hiding place,
we saw them handing the
bottle to someone.

Who was it?

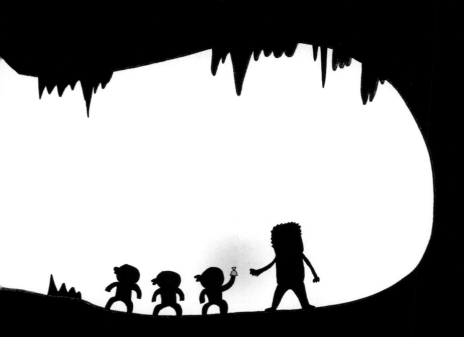

The man from the gym poster!

Remington-Hobbes!

He was standing in front of the stolen **Stotinki Trophy**, pouring a few precious drops of the **Egyptian Blue** into it.

"I now have **two** out of the **three** things I need to get the **Remington-Hobbes Trophy** back," he sneered.

"The **Silver Cup** and the **Egyptian Blue**!"

And then to our
horror, Devil-Cat
appeared beside him.

"What's next, sir?"

(OMG, he can talk!)

"Now all we need is **orange juice.**

Then I will be able to make a liquid that can melt bulletproof glass and bombproof concrete!

The Remington-Hobbes Trophy shall be **MINE** again!"

At last we knew what
was going on! But the
effects of the
freeze-bomb would
start wearing off
soon. We had to get
out of there, and fast.

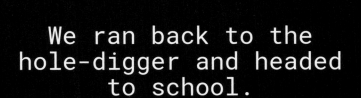

We ran back to the
hole-digger and headed
to school.

We got back to English
in the nick of time.

Mrs. Belch-Hick was
just unfreezing.

"And this is my favorite
part of the poem," she
continued.

"*The man looked at the
spoon, and then at the
moon...*"

Chapter 7

Paper Airplanes

Next up was
Paper Airplane class.

Definitely one of my favorites.

Our Paper Airplane teacher is **Mr. Hogsbottom.**

He actually works part-time as an *astronaut* and has been to the moon twice, and also once worked as a _triplocopter_ test *pilot*.

He's very good at making paper airplanes. Obviously.

But when we got to class,
we heard that he'd got
stung by a <u>grobsnot</u>
and was in bed for the
day (he must be allergic
to grobsnots)!

So we had a substitute teacher — a *strange*, tall lady who wouldn't let go of her two handbags and who knew nothing about paper airplanes.

She said we could just do whatever we wanted.

Perfect!

Rob and I had a mystery to solve.

What we knew so far:

① Remington-Hobbes wanted to get the Remington-Hobbes Trophy back.

② It was protected by a bulletproof cabinet on a bombproof plinth.

③ If he could get his hands on orange juice, he would be able to destroy the cabinet and plinth and get the trophy.

What we didn't know so far:

If he needed orange juice, why didn't he just go to a store and buy some?

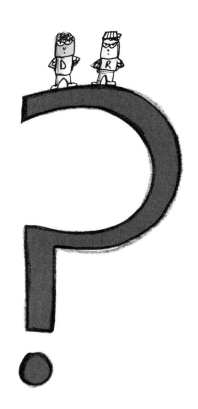

Come on, Dash,
think, think.

Then suddenly I
remembered something.

The *piece of paper* I'd
found at the cave and
put in my pocket!

Did I still have it?

Yes!

It was a **map** of a small part of the school, with crosses marked in three places.

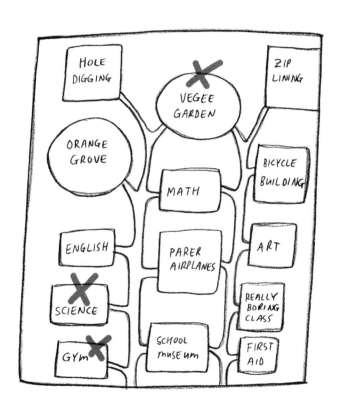

One **X** over the **gym** –
yes, that's where they
stole the silver trophy!

One **X** over **science lab** –
yes, that's where they
got the perfume from!

One **X** over the **vegetable
garden**??

If all he needed was orange juice, why was Remington-Hobbes interested in the vegetable garden?

Oranges grow in the **orange** grove, not the vegetable garden.

Aha!
Can you guess it?

Remington-Hobbes had sent Devil-Cat to steal CARROT 27b so that he could make CARROT JUICE!

The third ingredient!!

CARROT JUICE!

Possibly the only thing more orange than **orange juice!**

That was it!!

Rob and I grabbed our backpacks and **ran** to the vegetable garden as fast as we could.

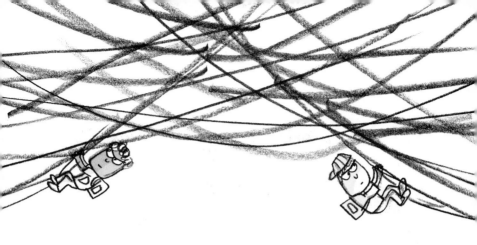

Once there, we set a trap.

A massive net of
krypto-web between
the trees.

Some quick facts
about krypto-web:

① World's strongest rope
② Made from hammaphore leaves
③ Holds in invisible things
④ Even saw-toothed doublodiles
can't bite through it.

Suddenly my KB-15
flashed and we
knew our enemies
were close.

Rob and I hid just in
time, and in they came.

Remington-Hobbes and
Devil-Cat and five
Wrestle-Scallywags.

171

They approached Carrot 27b.

"Okay, scallywags! You guard
us while we dig it out!"
ordered Remington-Hobbes.

And that's when we
released the net!

Bang on target!

We got them all.
Well, all except...Devil-Cat.
He'd managed to escape
AGAIN!

While I was securing the krypto-web, Rob pulled out his _SPIN radio_ and called for help.

Within thirty seconds,
a police
__triplo-triplocopter__
came hovering over
the school.

Remington-Hobbes and his gang were arrested and carried away.

Game over!

(In case you're interested,
they were taken to
Witch Nose Island,
the world's most secure
prison, where they remain.

For now.)

Meanwhile, we used
the warp-vortex to
get back to the cave
and recover the
Stotinki Trophy and
the Egyptian Blue.

When he saw we had the trophy, Mr. Grodzinsky was so happy that he started to cry.

And when she saw that we had her Egyptian Blue, Mrs. Tadros was so happy that she also started to cry.

Then
Mrs. Hogmanny-Hog-Mahomm
started to cry and so
did Mr. Darling.

And then
Gronville
Honkersmith
started to cry.

Things were beginning
to get a *little*
uncomfortable...

...but luckily the bell
rang and school was over
for the day.

Time to go home!

THE END!

Almanac

The COMPLETE ALMANAC is the place where you can find out everything about Dash and his world. It's online here: total-mayhem.com/almanac
This is the Book 1 Almanac, covering detailed information for this book only.

Anti-Invisibility Goggles

Anti-invisibility goggles (AIG) are an extremely useful tool. Dash and Rob usually carry them in their backpacks. They are most effective for recently invisibilized things. So for example, if a Wrestle-Scallywag went into invisibility mode a few minutes ago, the AIG would pick him up. But if they went into invisibility mode a few weeks ago, the AIG probably would not.

Backpack-Ladder

The backpack-ladder (BPL) is an important piece of equipment used by Dash and Rob on multiple missions. While very useful, it can also cause injury if incorrectly deployed. Accordingly, it is very important to have clear airspace over you when deploying. No low-lying trees or low ceilings, and obviously don't deploy inside an airplane, train, hovercraft, or hot-air balloon. The same goes for reverse deployment. Make sure there are no obstacles above you. When carrying one of these, make sure the top of your backpack is correctly fastened.

In 2016, three employees at the BPL factory were injured during the testing process. The main backpack cover was not correctly fastened and the ladder expanded inside the backpack, which then exploded. In 2019, a BPL auto-deployed in a factory staff member's car, causing him to drive off the road and into a shallow duck pond. Three ducks were injured, and the factory had to pay a $25,000 fine. All three ducks recovered.

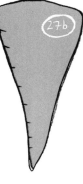

Carrot 27b

Famous for being the world's largest carrot. Estimated to be over ten feet long. And it's still growing.

Planted and grown by Mrs. Hogmanny-Hog-Mahomm, who is believed to have sung to it for over an hour every day, in its own language (Karrotsch).

She speaks over three hundred vegetable languages, and has actually translated the full Harry Potter series into Karrotsch. Very few people know this. She also read the books to Carrot 27b when it was still small.

Devil-Cat
Huge double-tailed black cat who always lands up on the wrong side of the law. Tends to partner with criminals. Fears nothing but fruit. Terrified of watermelons. However, he loves vegetables, especially carrots.

Drones
Dash uses a wide range of drones for communications and surveillance. Most are equipped with infra-red, infra-green, and infra-blue technology.

Freeze-Bombs
As the name suggests, these weapons freeze everything within fifty yards of the explosion. The effect lasts exactly fifteen minutes.

They can be really fun if you time them well. A freeze-bomb explodes two seconds after it's been thrown. If you time it just as someone is pouring a glass of water or about to jump into a pool, when the freeze effects wear off, it can be really funny.

Grobsnot
Nasty stinging insects a little like bees. Only left-handed people (like Mr. Hogsbottom and Mrs. Tadros) are allergic to them.

Hammaphore Tree
Several hammaphore trees grow in the forest next to Swedhump Elementary. Each one is said to be over five hundred years old. Every hammaphore tree has a secret doorway into a passage that

SECRET
DOORWAY

connects to all other hammaphore trees on the
planet. Dash and Rob are the only people who
know this. Or so it's believed.

Hole-Diggers

The two most common versions are the Aardvark 4.2d (used
by Dash and Rob) and the Aardvark 5.2rg (preferred by criminals).
The 4.2d has a 4.2-liter diesel
engine, but with a turboelectric
wassoon-emulsifier, so it's good
for stealth and speed. But it is not
great on endurance. The 5.2rg uses
regular gas and has a sprocket-glocken-
hemplekk-tekk at the rear, which is well
documented as being preferable for long missions.

KB-15

Imminent Danger Warning Device (IDWD)

KB-15 Flash Codes:
Red — on-off 1-second intervals
continuous: Imminent danger.
Red — on 2s, off 2s: Imminent
lightning storm.
Green — on 3s, off 1s: Takeout
delivery almost here.
Blue — on 5s, off 5s: Battery needs charging.

Krypto-Web

The world's strongest rope, it's made from the
leaf fibers of a hammaphore tree.
It's so strong that not even
a saw-toothed doublodile
can chew through it.

Move #6694 (Tower)

Used by Wrestle-Scallywags only.
Very technical three-scallywag move.
Typically Scallywag 1 jumps up, wall-bounces,
ceiling-bounces, and then lands to form the base.
Scallywag 2 jumps up, ceiling-bounces, floor-
bounces, and then lands on top of Scallywag 1.
Scallywag 3 jumps up and does an arc-soar to land on
Scallywag 2, thus forming the "Tower." They then
advance. Used primarily to intimidate opponents.
Its actual effectiveness is so far unproven.

Paper-Rock-Scissors-Carrot-Spoon-Tissue-Elbow
Similar to rock-paper-scissors (also known as ro-sham-bo).
This is a hand game played between two people in which each
player simultaneously forms one of seven
shapes with an outstretched hand.

It is a simultaneous, zero-sum game
insofar as it has only two possible
outcomes: a draw, or a win for one
player and a loss for the other.

Paper beats rock beats scissors beats carrot beats spoon beats
tissue (obviously) beats elbow beats paper.

Pinkfish
Like goldfish, but a different color. Pink, actually.
Very tame when happy, but when bored can be aggressive and bite
like piranhas.

Need constant attention, i.e., have to be walked,
entertained, read to before bed, etc. Some rich pinkfish
actually have their own walk-bowls. (Walk-bowls are
bowls that can walk, in case you were wondering.)

Quadcycles
Four-wheeled cycles that can fold up into a backpack and be
deployed by mind activation. The wheel configuration constantly
adapts to the terrain and is controlled by a very sophisticated
sensor (or "brain") embedded in the saddle. A quadcycle looks
easy to ride, but it is actually quite difficult.

A three-week introductory
course at the QTA (Quadcycle
Training Academy) is highly
recommended.

Quadcycle Maintenance:
Pretty much the same as a
regular bicycle maintenance,
apart from the sneggle-sprocket. Keep the drive-chain clean and
well lubricated, make sure brake-fluid pressure is good, check
all nuts and bolts before and after big missions, make sure the
tires are in good condition, and, finally, and most importantly,
make sure the sneggle-sprocket is smooth and has enough lemon
juice on it at all times. Make sure the lemon juice compression
canister is fully primed to at least level 8, especially before
big missions.

Saw-Toothed Doublodiles

Vicious nasty things that can cut through anything with their teeth. Except krypto-web. They can't cut through krypto-web. Some are vegetarian, while others are carnivorous (such as the flesh-eating saw-toothed dou-blodiles that breed around Witch Nose Island).

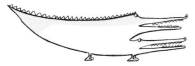

Scallywags

There are many different types of scallywag. Each type has its own fighting techniques, strengths, and weaknesses.

To officially become a scallywag, one needs to graduate from Scallywag Academy.

Secure Command Center (SCC)

The SCC is the technology headquarters for Dash and Rob. It's where their communications, surveillance, and airborne/waterborne reconnaissance hardware is stored and operated. It's only accessible by tunnel.

SPIN Radio

A SPIN radio (Secure Police Interface Neo-mogrifier) lets the user communicate directly with International Police Headquarters. Very few exist, and only highly trained experts are allowed to use them. It folds up to the size of a small pea. Rob Newman usually has one with him.

Stink-Balls

Stink-balls are thin-skinned capsules that get filled with gross liquid known as stink-ball juice. It is possible to brew your own. Stink-ball capsules (SBCs) can be purchased from your local Spyware & Rockets store.

Typical stink-ball ingredients include:
* Rotting hammaphore fruit
* Old fish tank water
* Rotting guacamole
* Doublodile saliva
* Grobsnot venom
* Sour walrus milk
* Fresh swed milk
* Pickled fungus
* Slug slime
* Liver

Brew for one month on a cast-iron pot over a fire made from the bark of a hammaphore tree.

Once brewed, let chill, and then fill the capsules. Be sure to seal capsules properly so they don't leak in your backpack or holster.

Swedhump Elementary
Dash's school.
Principal: Mrs. Rosebank.
Probably the best school in the world.
Definitely has the best teachers in the world.
Named after the hump of
a swed, a two-faced
humped creature.

Transformer
A transformer is a HIGHLY technical device. There are over one hundred different types, and new models come out each year. Dash currently uses a Chobey-2021.

If you have FULL security clearance (level 15c), we will be able to tell you more. Dash's transformer uses an RM66 high-voltage battery, which needs to be charged once a week. No more, no less. If charged more often that that, the transformer becomes too powerful. So for example, if overcharged when trying to transform a cereal bowl into a watermelon, it could actually transform it into a hippopotamus, which would be funny, but probably not good. If charged less often than weekly, the transformer becomes too weak. So for example, if you wanted to transform a bicycle into a car, it might transform it into a wheelbarrow instead.

Triplocopter

Triple-helicopters invented by G. & J.
Tarrow Siblings Inc. in 2010. The equivalent
of three helicopters stuck together. They
are sixty-one times faster and seventeen
times more powerful than regular helicopters, though more complicated to fly. The
test pilot of the first version was James
Hogsbottom, who teaches Paper Airplane
class at Swedhump Elementary. There have
been no reported triplocopter crashes
to date.

Triplo-Triplocopter

These are simply triple triplocopters,
i.e., the equivalent of nine helicopters
stuck together. Super fast and powerful,
but can only be flown by the very top
students at flight school. James
Hogsbottom was the first person to ever
successfully land one. There have been
three documented triplo-triplocopter crashes
to date.

VAMP Transponder

The VAMP (Voice Amplification Modification and
Projection) transponder, a highly sophisticated,
tiny device, has three functions:
[1] Modification: Allows the user to change his or
her own voice into someone else's.
[2] Amplification: Makes the user's voice louder.
[3] Projection: Allows the user's voice to travel greater dis-
tances and faster.
VAMP transponders can be embedded in other devices. Dash has one
embedded in his anti-invisibility goggles. Manufactured by
Mgadigadi Technologies. Earring versions are available, but they
are fragile.

Warp-Vortex

A warp-vortex allows the warpee (owner)
plus sub-warpees (passengers) to move from
one place to another in a trilli-second.
Warp-vortexes are typically backpack-
mounted. Pocket versions do exist but are
quite expensive.

Each warp-vortex has its own password, which the users will not
share under any circumstances (so don't even ask).

Witch Nose Island

Witch Nose Island is the most secure prison on earth.
The entire perimeter is ringed by twenty-seven
krypto-web fences, eleven of which are electrified. The water
around it is freezing and full of shnarks (which are
more vicious than sharks), flesh-eating saw-toothed
doublodiles, and killer electric rays.

No prisoner has ever escaped from it.

Wobble-Ball

Sport that involves racing around a room while balancing atop
a big wobbly rubber ball. Invented by Sir Stephenson
Remington-Hobbes in 2012.

List of Wobble-Ball World Champions
Year 1: Sir Stephenson Remington-Hobbes
Year 2: Sir Stephenson Remington-Hobbes
Year 3: Sir Stephenson Remington-Hobbes
Year 4: Sir Stephenson Remington-Hobbes
Year 5: Mr. Grodzinsky
Year 6: Mr. Grodzinsky
Year 7: Mr. Grodzinsky
Year 8: Mr. Grodzinsky

Wombat Juice

Wombat juice actually has nothing to do with wombats.

The name comes from its ingredients:
Walrus milk
Octopus saliva
Mango
Beetroot
Avocado
Tomato

Blend them in any proportions,
then serve with ice. Delicious!

Wrestle-Scallywags

How common: Very.
Special power: None. Decent all-rounders.
Weakness: Poor eyesight.
Typical group size: 3 or more.
Operate alone? Hardly ever.
Maximum jump distance: 16 feet.
Cleverness: 5/10.
Speed: 5/10.
Agility: 9.5/10.

Yo-Yo Stingers

Yo-yo stingers are electrically charged yo-yos.
When fighting scallywags, they can be very effective, but
they only sting for a few seconds. They are best used to
give someone a fright. If you're involved in deep combat
with a full squad of scallywags, for instance, it's worth
having multiple yo-yo stingers with you.

This is the end of this book's Almanac.
*For the **complete Almanac**, go to:*

www.total-mayhem.com

FOR DASH CANDOO, EVERY DAY IS . . .

TOTAL MAYHEM!

ABOUT THE CREATORS

Ralph Lazar and Lisa Swerling live in California.

Ralph made up the Dash stories (inspired by wrestling his godson — Dash!) and did the drawings. Lisa shaped the stories into this book.

Ralph and Lisa are New York Times *bestselling authors, and the creators of the popular illustrated project* Happiness Is..., *which has been translated into over twenty languages and has over three million followers online.*